Reverence

Caleb's Lost Chapters

A Significance Series Novella

SHELLY CRANE

Editing services provided by Jennifer Nunez.

Available in paperback and Kindle and E-book format through Amazon and Barnes & Noble, Smashwords and Createspace.

More information can be found at the author's website
http://shellycrane.blogspot.com/

ISBN- 13 978-1477585542
ISBN-10: 1477585540

One

Significance Chapter Four

I woke up with a jackhammer in my spine. At first I thought it was just Kyle's crappy spare bed, but it wasn't. It was withdrawals. Withdrawals from my Maggie because I had imprinted. And her heart was banging around in my chest.

I couldn't even make myself get out of bed. I just lay there and remembered everything from the night before. It was all real. The girl at the bus stop, her saving me from the jackass in the truck, her being beautiful and awesome, her touching me...she was mine.

I jerked up out of bed with a renewed vigor, but quickly slowed a retreat as my back groaned and protested like an old person's. "Ah," I groaned to no one. "Holy hell."

"Caleb?" I heard through the door. "Are you awake yet, boy?"

"Yeah," I answered gruffly and ran a hand through my hair of spikes as Gran came inside the door and put her hands on her hips as she grinned at me. "What?" I asked in the most reserved voice I could to show that I was annoyed, but still be respectful.

"You're bent over like an eighty year old and groaning and complaining through the walls. You still giddy that you imprinted?"

"Of course I am, Gran," I said quietly. I blew a breath and leaned my elbows on my knees. "I will admit that the withdrawals suck, though."

"That they do," she agreed and came to sit on the bed with me. "The sooner you get to her, the better you'll feel."

"Yeah, but I don't want to scare her. If I run over there before a decent hour, she'll probably freak and kick me out."

"I highly doubt that, boy." She lifted a piece of hair from next to my ear in her fingers. "Girls usually invite cute boys *in*, not throw them out."

"Maybe, but I want to be absolutely sure that she's ready. I'll go, but I want her to have a minute to wake up and catch her breath first. Today is going to be really crazy for her."

"Well, I'll leave you to get ready, I guess." She stood and looked down at me. "She'll have to get used to crazy if she's gonna be with us."

I laughed. "Let's ease her into it, Gran."

"If you say so," she cackled and made her way out.

"Please, please, Gran. Take it easy on her."

Her cackle was not reassuring as it got louder. As soon as she was gone, I threw my clothes on and went down the hall to bang on Kyle's door.

He was my key to opening the door labeled 'Maggie'.

"Kyle, I know you hear me banging away out here. Open the door, slacker."

I heard his growl through the door, "I'll murder you and claim insanity if you don't scram."

"Kyle, open up. What kind of weirdo locks his bedroom door anyway?"

"The kind that has jerks staying over who steal girlfriends."

I pressed my fingers into my eyes and took a deep breath as the pain in my back and legs got a little worse. "She wasn't your girlfriend."

"Irrelevant!" he yelled, but I heard movement on the other side. He yanked the door open and glared at me. He was wearing nothing but plaid boxers and his hair was a serious mess. The pillow lines on his face completely disarmed his scowl. "What, Cuz? Wanna steal my wallet, too?"

"Dude," I drawled and pushed him out of the way so I could enter. "What is wrong with you?"

"I thought it was obvious," he said sarcastically and threw himself back on the bed and slammed the covers over his head.

"It's not, actually." I pulled his desk chair over and straddled it, resting my arms along the back. I rubbed my eyes again, hoping to stave off the pain behind them a little. "I don't care who the girl was, if you imprinted on someone, I'd be happy for you."

"Not if you were trying to date her, you wouldn't," he said, his voice muffled from the blanket.

I yanked the blanket back and punched his leg lightly. "I told you it was a bad idea to even try."

"Whatever," he muttered and stayed right where he was, arms wide and face turned away from me on the mattress.

"Come on, man. I'm about to go get her. I need you to give me her address."

"Not a chance." He turned his head to glare at me some more. "Why would I help you with her?"

"Because this sucks, bro." I rubbed my neck. "The withdrawals ain't no joke."

"Boo hoo. Cry me a freaking river."

"Maggie's hurting as bad as me, or worse." He stiffened. "Come on, help me."

He stayed still and silent, but then exhaled and rolled over again. "Fine."

He spouted the street address and before he was even done, I was gone. I could feel her heartbeat, and it was getting stronger in my chest, and I knew that it would lead me to her if she was distressed anyway. So after brushing my teeth and swiping my hair back with my fingers, I hit the pavement without saying another word to anyone.

As I walked, I passed the stoplight where she saved me last night, right as her heartbeat kicked into high gear right next to mine. My feet took off before my brain even understood what was going on.

It was strange how I knew right where to go; no guessing, no tripping feet, no veering. I went right into the front door of a house that I'd never seen, went up the stairs to a bathroom door, opened it and took the girl in my arms.

Immediately a sigh escaped us both and I could feel again. Breathe again. Gah, she smelled so good. I ran my hand up her arm to fill her with my touch. "I'm sorry," I whispered to her. "I got here as fast as I could."

I didn't want to rush her or scare her, and she needed my touch whether she wanted it or not, but she leaned into me and accepted everything I had to offer. I felt everything inside of me relax.

I actually sniffed her hair as I continued to hold her to me. I had to figure out what that smell was, but it could wait. As she leaned back to look at me, anything I might have been thinking was lost to me.

Holy….she was absolutely gorgeous, even more so than last night. Her freckles were spackles of cuteness across her nose. And the blue shirt she was wearing was soft and see-through across her shoulders. I gulped to keep from saying something stupid. Like how much my body was screaming to kiss her, throw her over my shoulder and take her away from everyone and everything, never ever stop touching her.

"Hi," she said, her voice breathy and sweet from toothpaste.

"Hi," I answered back and my cheeks hurt. I realized I was grinning like a frigging idiot and started doing something else to distract myself. I pushed her hair back to inspect the wound...that I had inflicted on her. Man, that hurt to think about.

"How's the head?" I asked.

"It's fine. It doesn't hurt anymore."

"Did you sleep ok?"

"Yeah. I slept great, actually."

I realized that I still had her in my arms, all cave man like, and promptly stepped back to give her a little space. I wanted her to be comfortable, even if that meant that I wasn't touching her.

"And I was fine, I mean I felt a little weird, like I had the flu," she said and I nodded to confirm, "but it wasn't until I started to think about things- um, you, that I freaked."

"I know. It happens, especially the first few days after an imprinting."

"Why?"

I shrugged and tried to speak clearly. "Doesn't matter. I'm here now, and I have no intentions of going very far."

"Good," she answered, her green eyes locked on mine. I grinned, couldn't be helped. She swallowed delicately, her throat working down her neck. Ah...gah....

I asked her about going out with Kyle. Then all hell broke loose in my body. I saw the offense mark, in my mind it was like I gripped her and slung her around I was so angry, but I didn't. My touch was gentle and she was calming *me* down. Some. But it was then that I realized she was just as strong and capable as I was of

9

being there. Of being kind and gentle and just...there when you needed them. I didn't know if she understood what her touch was doing for me or not, but she was like a band-aid to my pissy mood.

Then I seemed to come back into myself as I heard the name of the Watson who'd always wanted to kick my teeth in. "Marcus touched you?" I asked softly, running my finger along her smooth skin. She was so breakable and had no idea the sadistic things Marcus was capable of.

"He grabbed me when we tried to walk away. But as soon as he knew that I- you- we..."

"That we imprinted," I supplied, my grin now fixed back into position. I held back my growl of satisfaction. Barely.

"Yes. He left. I didn't see this until this morning."

"It's what happens to warn them that you don't belong to them."

"I know, I felt it, but why didn't it do that when Kyle touched me?"

"Kyle touched you?" I asked and once again felt my blood begin to warm to uncomfortable levels in my veins.

"He held my hand a couple times," she explained. "Mostly to make me keep up with him, but it never did that with him."

"It only happens if the person's actions aren't of pure intention. Your body can sense it when someone means you harm."

"So, that Marcus guy wanted to hurt me?" she said all breathy and vulnerable.

"Don't worry about that just yet." I got bold and brought my hand to her cheek. My big ugly hand next to her gorgeous face seemed strange...but right. "One thing at a time. I'll explain it all to you, but right now, I need to get you over to Kyle's. My family is all there, waiting for us."

"Eh," she groaned. "I don't like crowds."

"You'll like this crowd." I smiled to reassure her, and the thought of my family meeting her and this becoming seriously real was the best thing I could think of at the time. "They were so happy last night when I told them what happened. They can't wait to meet you."

So she took me downstairs, I met her father who barely spared her a glance and then walked with her to Kyle's. Even though I wasn't touching her, I knew she was scared. Her heart was beating fast in my chest. And I was scared. What if she met my big, crazy family and bolted? What if once she knew all the facts, she wanted nothing to do with any of it. Or me? What if Gran's inappropriate comments were too much for this girl whose mom left and dad checked out of her life?

She stopped on the lawn and I knew she was freaking out. I had to fight my hands to stay where they were while she ranted and tried to convince me she was a nobody, nothing, worthless. I'd never wanted to strangle anyone as badly as I wanted to strangle her parents for making her feel that way about herself.

I stepped to her, and on a wing and a prayer, put my arm around her lower back, lifting her face with a finger under her chin. I waited for her to push me off, or slap me even for being bold, but she just looked at me and waited for whatever I might have to say. It was enough to inflate my ego a little bit, I'll admit, but I kept my grin to myself and explained to her about imprints, about my family, about how I chose her and had no regrets.

"There is nothing that can change or break that. And even if there was, I wouldn't want to. Not for the world." I moved my hand to her cheek once more and felt along her cheek bone with my thumb. I could have stood there all day with her looking at me like that. "I've seen you. You can't fake or glimmer what's inside your mind. And you are sweet and caring and absolutely lovable in that head of yours. I promise you my family will love you. In fact, I'm sure they already do. You're one of us now and they can sense how I feel about you."

"How you feel about me," she repeated and smiled like it was private. I felt her...joy... Oh, man. I smiled, too. "This is all so strange," she said breathlessly.

11

"Just wait," I leaned in to whisper in her ear. "It'll only get stranger." I heard my husky chuckle and once again thought maybe she'd revolt and push me away. But no, she just waited, her heart thumping for more reasons than one. And I frigging loved it. "Come on. If you're ready, let's go on in so everyone will stop staring out the window."

After she knew we were caught, the blush that crept up her cheeks was adorable and I fell in love with her a little bit right there on the lawn. Right there on Uncle Ken's ridiculously manicured lawn, I knew that my life was over and a new life was beginning.

One where the girl in my arms was all mine, in every way, and I waited patiently at her feet for a chance to do anything she asked of me.

Two

Accordance Chapter Ten

I woke up on the beach with my hands searching for what they always did in the morning. They didn't have to look far as she was situated on my lap nicely. Then I heard Maggie talking. I peeked my eyes open to ease my vision into the sun and saw Bella eating up Maggie's attention.

My two girls, getting along and loving on each other.

"She really has taken to you," I said, causing Maggie to jump. She smiled up at me before turning her attention back to Bella.

"Yeah, she has. She's a sweet girl. Us girls gotta stick together, don't we?"

"I'm trying not to be jealous."

"Jealous of me or Bella?" she said, her little smile playful. She was still planted on my lap facing me, her hair a beautiful mess of curls around her face under the hoodie. She had no makeup on, no qualms about it either. Gah, she was

14

absolutely gorgeous like this. I flexed my fingers, searching for her body that I knew was under all that fabric of my hoodie she was wearing.

"Either," I answered quietly and watched her face as I leaned in for what I wanted. She giggled and bit her lip, leaning in, too. But Bella stuck her jealous nose right in between us. Maggie laughed as I pushed Bella away playfully. "Alright, you. Go lay down."

She trotted off somewhere, but I kept my eyes on Maggie. Or her lips I should say. I gripped the back of her neck gently and brought her mouth to mine, because I was done waiting. She let me lead her and her being pliant and willing for me always was fan-frigging-tastic.

I pulled back to give her a second to breath. "Good morning."

"Morning," she breathed and licked her bottom lip…as if in a daze. I almost groaned.

"So, did you like sleeping on the beach?"

"Yeah." She pulled down her hood and I smoothed her hair for her. "I love the beach." She snuggled back into my chest. "Can we move here? Buy a little yellow beach house with a wraparound porch and just never leave?"

I sighed and tried to breathe passed the punch in my gut. Wasn't that exactly what I wanted? She always seemed so reluctant to talk about marrying me, moving in with me, anything about our future really. I didn't understand it, and as much as I didn't want to push her, I didn't understand why she didn't want those things with me. So to hear her say that…

"I will do whatever it takes," I said softly into her hair, "to get you to move in with me. Anything you'll let me do if you'll allow me to take care of you the way I was meant to. I want to buy you a house, and if I have to move to California to do it, I will."

She looked up at me and I listened to her internal rant. She had her reasons for feeling the way she did. Her mom, if you could call her that, had abandoned her. Her parents hadn't exactly set a good example. Maggie was so young. I got all

15

her reasons, but I wanted her. I wanted her to let me take care of her the way my body was demanding me to.

And then I heard her inner thought that had my heart racing, my mouth suddenly dry and empty of words, and my head floating, my body humming with possibilities.

Wow, I was being so stupid. The answer was right there in front of me. Marry the man. Live with him and be happy and prosper. Why was I being such a silly idiot about it all?

She looked up at me, all full of innocence and love…for me. I sighed harshly and took that gorgeous, soft face in my hands, saying the one thing that I'd wanted to ask her since I first felt her skin on mine. "Maggie, marry-"

Bella's bark cut me off and I growled inside. Could a guy get a frigging break? I smiled at Maggie as much as I could, not wanting her to think I was upset. Though if she dug far enough, she'd know. And now Kyle and the bimbo, as Maggie referred to her in her mind, were making a lazy path to us.

Maggie tucked herself into my chest - burrowed in was more like it - and thought about all kinds of things as I bantered with Kyle back and forth. She didn't know I was listening to her and Kyle both, and she let her mind wander. She was serene, but determined.

Then Amber started throwing a hissy because Bella licked her hand. And Maggie came to her rescue.

"She's not disgusting," she sang to Bella. "You're a sweet, big girl." She looked up at Amber as I couldn't take my eyes off of her. "She's really sweet and soft and lovey. She can't help it she's so fluffy."

I watched her as she defended and soothed Bella as if she was her own. If there had been some kind of proverbial last straw or final inch that I was waiting for, this was it. I didn't care what happened to us; somehow, someway, I was going to marry this girl.

16

Kyle and Amber sauntered off after Kyle's half refusal to take her home. Wow, what a jerkface.

"He's just a normal, human teenage boy. That's how they act," she said, ever ready to defend her lifelong friend, Kyle.

"I never did," I countered.

"Yes," she put my arms around my neck, "but you were waiting for me, remember?" she said sweetly and smiled up at me.

"Mmhmm," I heard myself murmur as I pressed her lips to mine, sucking on the top then the bottom before taking them completely, like it was my right. "And now I've got you."

It took no amount of persuasion as she melted against me and let me take her tongue. My body was growling and howling like some animal on the inside. She never plundered my mind, never went in deep and tried to find all my nooks and crannies. She played along the surface. I think she was scared of what she'd find, and she was probably right about that. Because my body was a demanding beast that needed her, wanted her, had to have her and protect her at all cost to anyone or anything. Like now.

If she went into my thoughts now, she'd see that I was gripping the ledge of control and howling with the satisfaction of feeling and seeing her response to me. And when she groaned against my mouth, her little hands gripping my neck and hair, it was all I could do to stay put, refuse to throw her over my shoulder and cart her to the house.

And then there she was, in my head, sliding her way in and trying to meld our minds. Boy, was I tempted. I let her in for a few minutes- like I had a choice as she slammed her way past my barriers. I saw things in her mind as I always did when we melded our minds. There was one of me playing guitar and she was watching my arms as they held the bass and the muscles rippled. I think she probably embellished on that a little bit and I laughed inside.

I saw us on the plane together, but I was asleep. She dug through my brain, on a mission to be just as proactive as me when it came to learning about her. She found all sorts of things and I loved how much she loved it.

Then I saw her favorite memory of me, the one I saw every single time I entered her mind; the day we imprinted, and I was looking at her like she was my everything, because she was. I had looked at her face so closely that day, loving everything there was; freckles, green honest eyes, a mouth that was as perfect as it was dangerous.

She also saw my favorite memories of her, but when she went deeper, I pulled back, I held my control.

I pressed my head to hers and was surprised by how much my breathing was crazy. So it seemed she affected me just as much as I her. Well didn't that just bring a grin to my smug face...

"You can dig in my mind anytime you want, babe, but not like this," I said as sternly as I could, but chuckled instead when I saw her flushed face. "I want to, you know I do, especially since we were so close last time and were interrupted. I don't think I could stand to start and not...finish again, ok? Let's just wait until we know we won't have any distractions."

She started thinking all sorts of things to get my blood boiling again. I pulled her to stand.

"I better get you inside," I said into her ear, "before you convince me that the public beach is an appropriate place for such a thing." I nipped her earlobe.

"Caleb," she breathed, her fingers digging into my shirt front, "that's not helping."

"I know," I said and laughed as she swatted at me. Oh, I did know exactly what buttons to push. And I had no intentions of stopping anytime soon.

She was mine. All mine.

Three

Defiance Chapter Thirteen

I had never been in the cells myself, but I knew it was bad down there. And when they brought me down the steps, the smell of mold and stench choking me, I knew I wasn't going to be impressed with the place.

Then they took my shoes off and made me walk on the disgusting floor to my cell. I felt stuff crunching under my feet. I assumed it was bones or trash of some kind, but tried not to think about it. I sat in the cell and just waited…for something, anything, because there was nothing but a cot in there. Not even light enough to see, just enough to tease my senses from the guards lamp down the hall.

I didn't sleep because I just couldn't. Then I felt Maggie's heart skip. I sat up at attention and inquired about it. She said it was a spider, which was an appalling attempt to lie, but she slammed her mind shut and kicked me out.

That's when I knew she was up to something. My legs twitched uncomfortably with the need to make sure she was safe and not up to anything that would get her hurt. But I was useless in here, wasn't I?

I knew it was going to happen, but that didn't make me like any of it more, and knowing that Maggie was wandering around out there on a rescue mission was making everything worse. So I sat there simmering in my pity party.

A while later I felt her and knew she was close. My veins screamed at me to get her away from here.

Maggie, dang it, get your butt out of here!

No, Caleb. I'm already here. May as well see the accommodations.

I growled and banged my fist against the wall. If they touched one hair on her head, I'd...I jerked up to the bars and shook the door latch in vain, knowing full well that they charmed it. Like they did everything else. Cowards.

Then I heard her, and just her voice was like a punch to my core. I leaned against the bars, but still couldn't see her yet. She was arguing with Donald. I waited, angry and anxious. It wasn't like she was in mortal danger, I knew that, but it was just the fact that I was helpless in this cell and if she had been in danger, I wouldn't be able to do anything about it.

But when she charged down the hall towards me, and I saw in her mind how Donald had ran away like a weasel, my anger slipped away and pride took its place. Gah, she was amazing...

The smile that lit her face was gorgeous as she reached me and I held her face through the bars. I hadn't even realized we'd already begun to withdraw until her skin shot me a dose of relief. I'd been so worried about her, I'd forgotten all about anything that was happening to me.

"Open it," I said, my voice gravelly and grated.

"Keys?" she asked.

21

"They don't use keys down here, babe," I explained. I motioned to the bars to show her there was no lock. She pulled on the door, but it wouldn't move. She looked at me questioningly, biting her lip. "It's charmed."

She huffed, the energy ribbons starting to glow around us, so I explained how to get the door open. She slammed the door on the other side, having to sidestep so as not to be crushed. I held my curse in and engulfed her in my arms, breathing her in. She smelled heavenly, and I probably smelled like a sewer, but didn't care right then.

"Mmm, you're in so much trouble," I said to her, but she knew my threat was ridiculous, given by the grin on my face. "You refuse to listen, don't you?"

"When it's about you and jail? Yes." She grinned back at me. "Come on, gorgeous, let's go."

"Hey, that's my line," I said, but stepped on something and jolted. I refused to look down at what it was, but Maggie was already ahead of me. She got all in a tizzy, her heart spiking at the thought of my being hurt.

It was pretty hot.

All I wanted to do was get her back to her room. So after we went round with Aleza, I finally got her where I wanted her. I pulled her into her room like I owned the joint and went straight to the shower. I left the door open absolutely on purpose, knowing that Maggie hadn't followed me in. I pulled my shirt off, the smell of the cell all over it made me want to throw it in the trash. I tossed it away, unbuttoned my jeans and started the water, almost all the way hot. I felt Maggie's innocent interest slam into me. I imagined her in my mind as she watched me, not sure what was going to happen next.

So I turned to look at her. The look in her eyes, on her face, the way her heart seemed to slow down and her breath held...like she was waiting for something. I let my jeans fall and noticed the delicate gulp and ripple of her throat.

So I gave her the option to look or not. And I wasn't surprised in the slightest as I hooked my fingers into the waistband of my boxers, and pulled down...she waited until the last second and shut her eyes tightly.

22

I chuckled to myself as I got in the shower. She was the same girl she was when I met her. No matter all the crazy things that had happened to us, she was still herself. And I was in love with that girl out there, every bit and piece of her.

I knew when she came into the bathroom. Even though I couldn't feel her or read her mind because of the charmed room, I knew exactly where she was. I heard the water running, but resisted the urge to peek out of the curtain.

When I finished, I dried off and wrapped the towel around my hips. The curtain drew back and she was brushing her teeth. I was floored at how adorable it was. And sexy. Who knew brushing your teeth could be so sexy?

I joined her and watched her as she finished. Then I decided to brush mine as well and tamped down on my grin as she watched me as I had watched her. When I was done she kissed my chin and I grimaced, knowing I needed a shave. I went to the shower and grabbed the razor I'd seen in there from before. She watched enthralled as I did the job. When I was done with that, too, I poked my chin out to her for inspection.

She touched me, then kissed me, all sultry like, and put her cheek to mine. We were at such ease with each other, but there was still a nervous friction there as well.

I wrapped my arms around her middle and pressed my ear to her chest. With the charmed room, I was missing our connection. It felt wrong, completely wrong, to not have her in my head. I listened to her heart beat steadily as she ran her fingers through my hair.

"The sound of your heartbeat…is my favorite sound in the whole world." Then I drifted up and planted a kiss on the side of her neck. She gasped the startled, lovely sound that I knew she would. "And that is my second favorite sound," I said, all smug and happy. Then I lifted my head to look at her.

"I didn't say thank you for coming to save me," I said softly.

"I didn't think you would," she answered.

"I'm not mad," I said even softer so that she knew I was serious, "I just hate that you had to do that. I hate that you're seeing all the bad parts of my people and none of the good."

She tried to soothe me and explain it away, but none of that really mattered. I was just ready for bed…and maybe a little bit more than that. I murmured something about changing and she scurried away like a shot. I laughed as I dropped the towel and put on my boxers once again.

I emerged into the room and went right to turn the lights off. Though we couldn't feel anything but our skin when we touched - no healing, no tingles, no shots of calm - I still needed to be with her. I needed to feel her in any way that I could.

So I walked right to her in the dark as if my body knew where to find her anywhere. I collided with her gently and pushed her to the bed. She giggled against my lips at my enthusiasm before settling into her own need for me, just as strong.

After long, good minutes of kissing her senseless and being owned by a mouth that I didn't even realized I'd missed so much, I pulled her to lay against the pillows with me. We talked about the charmed room and how it was kind of nice to get a break from each other's thoughts. Then we talked about how she was absolutely, no going back, one of us now.

And even though I didn't think it was possible, as we eased back on the pillows once more and she snuggled in against me, I fell in love with her a little bit more.

Independence

Sneak Peek

Caleb came up behind me as I stood in his apartment in front of the stove. "You cooked supper?" he asked and sniffed the air over my shoulder from behind. "Smells good."

"It's your mom's Shepherd's Pie," I explained and turned to him. "She gave me the recipe and a few pointers."

"I'm sure it's awesome," he murmured and kissed my neck before making his way to my lips. "Did you get anything else done today?" He grinned. "Wedding wise?"

"Gran fitted me for my dress," I said and sighed. "It's so unbelievably beautiful."

"I can't wait to see it," he replied in a husky tone. "For now, I'll settle with fruit shorts." He squeezed my hips in his hands. "Bananas tonight, huh?"

"Yeah," I breathed as he inched closer. "I heard they were your favorite."

"To be absolutely honest, Maggie," he stopped when there was no more space between us, just cotton and denim separated all of him from all of me, "they are my favorite."

And then supper was forgotten.

You can follow Shelly at these venues

www.shellycrane.blogspot.com

www.facebook.com\shellycranefanpage

Twitter @authshellycrane

6325487R00018

Made in the USA
San Bernardino, CA
06 December 2013